It started off as quite an ordinary day in the jungle. The birds were singing their morning songs. Momma Elephant and her children were coming home from brushing their tusks beside the river.

Tiger and his wife were having
breakfast.

The Strange Bird

Adele Geras

Illustrated by

J.   S A 38255

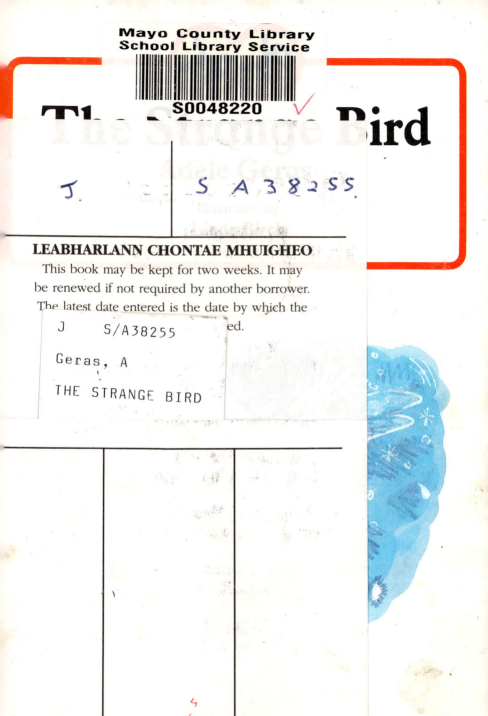

HAMISH HAMILTON CHILDREN'S BOOKS

Published by the Penguin Group
27 Wrights Lane, London W8 5TZ, England
Viking Penguin Inc., 40 West 23rd Street, New York, New York 10010, U.S.A.
Penguin Books Australia Ltd, Ringwood, Victoria, Australia
Penguin Books Canada Ltd, 2801 John Street, Markham, Ontario, Canada L3R 1B4
Penguin Books (N.Z.) Ltd, 182–190 Wairau Road, Auckland 10, New Zealand

Penguin Books Ltd, Registered Offices, Harmondsworth, Middlesex, England

First published in Great Britain 1988 by
Hamish Hamilton Children's Books

British Library Cataloguing in Publication Data
Geras, Adèle
The strange bird.
I. Title
823'.914[J]   PZ7

ISBN 0–241–12261–9

Typeset by Kalligraphics Ltd, Redhill, Surrey
Printed in Great Britain by
Cambus Litho Ltd,
East Kilbride, Scotland

Giraffe was just setting out to visit
Leopard when he noticed a strange bird
sitting on a branch of the jacaranda tree.

"I've never seen a bird like that before,"
said Giraffe. "It's shiny. Birds aren't
supposed to be shiny, are they, Momma
Elephant?"

"Certainly not," said Momma
Elephant, peering up at the tree. "It looks
dangerous to me, with that sharp beak.
Little Six, go and fetch Tiger and
Leopard here at once. We should decide
what's to be done about it."

Little Six was back very quickly, with Tiger and his wife and Leopard huffing and puffing anxiously behind her.

Tiger whispered, "I expect it's foreign. I've certainly never seen a bird like that in this jungle. Perhaps we should all approach it together. Can't be too careful, you know. Got to find out if it's friendly."

Leopard said, "I don't like the way the sunlight bounces off its back. It dazzles you just to look at it."

"If everybody's here," said Momma Elephant, "we should gather round it together. It wouldn't dare to attack so many of us. Come along, all of you, form a straight line behind me."

All the animals grouped together according to size, and the birds and butterflies flew along overhead.

The strange bird did not move, but sat quietly on its branch.

"Excuse me," said Momma Elephant, "but we would like to know who you are and where you come from and especially whether you are friendly. We've never seen a bird quite like you before and we're all a little worried."

The strange bird spoke, "Please do not worry. I am a Mirror Bird and I come from Mirror Bird Mountain, which lies across the ocean. I have heard that this is a very pleasant jungle, so I have come to see it for myself. I mean you no harm."

"That's all very well," said Leopard, "but what is a mirror?"

"A mirror," said the strange bird, " is a glass in which you can see yourself. Come closer."

15

Gingerly, the animals made a circle around the tree. The Mirror Bird flew down to the lowest branch and one by one the animals looked into the thousands of mirrors that sparkled on its breast and its wings.

"Goodness," said Giraffe, "is that
really me? My neck does stretch on and
on, doesn't it?"

Tiger said to his wife, "Our stripes are really rather handsome, don't you think?"

"See how long and coiled I am!" said
Snake. "I never realised."

"I am far more wrinkled than I thought. Perhaps I shouldn't frown so much," sighed Momma Elephant. "But my ears are still magnificent."

"We are even prettier than we thought we were," said the butterflies.

"We think we're even prettier than you are," said the birds.

21

Leopard looked into the mirror. "I think I look rather tired. I shall take a small snooze. Thank you, Mirror Bird."

"It seems to me," said Momma Elephant, "that you are going to be a great help to everyone. You can show us all what we are like, and teach us things about ourselves that we didn't know before. You're most welcome in our jungle."

All the animals were now very eager to show the Mirror Bird around the jungle.

"You are very beautiful," sang the birds as they flew with the Mirror Bird over the twisting, silver river that ran through the jungle. "Quite different from us, of course, but very beautiful."

"We must apologise," said Tiger, offering the Mirror Bird some fruit as they visited his home, "if we frightened you, all marching up to you like that. But you frightened us too, you know! We'd be honoured if you would like to stay in our jungle."

"Can my friends come too?" asked the Mirror Bird.

"Of course," said Giraffe, as they walked around his tall house, "there's plenty of room for everyone here."

"Certainly there is," said Momma
Elephant, as she hurried to find her guest
a perch. "I'm sorry we were rude to you at
first. You are to make yourself completely
at home."

She pushed her children into a line.

"Go and see that your ears are tidily placed. There's no excuse for looking untidy now we have the Mirror Bird with us," she smiled.

The little elephants did as they were told, and then the Mirror Bird flew to the top of the jacaranda tree and started building her nest.